A Brief Natural History of Women

Sarah Freligh

Harbor Editions
Small Harbor Publishing

A Brief Natural History of Women
Copyright © 2023 SARAH FRELIGH
All rights reserved.

Cover art "I Walked Away and Started a New Life" by Stacy Russo
Cover design by Allison Blevins
Book layout by Allison Blevins and Hannah Martin

A BRIEF NATURAL HISTORY OF WOMEN
SARAH FRELIGH
ISBN 978-1-957248-13-4
Harbor Editions,
an imprint of Small Harbor Publishing

Contents

You Come Here Often / 9

A Brief Natural History of How It Is to Be a Girl / 11

A Brief Natural History of Lipstick / 12

Girl Talk / 13

A Brief Natural History of Mothers / 14

Reunion / 15

Oh, the Water / 20

The Thing With Feathers / 23

A Brief Natural History of Our Fathers / 26

That Girl / 29

A Brief Natural History of the Other Woman / 30

A Brief Natural History of Babies, Because / 31

In Real Life / 32

All We Wanted / 34

Your Life as a Bottle / 35

A Brief Natural History of the Automobile / 36

Saginaw / 40

Other Tongues / 41

A Brief Natural History of *Law and Order* / 44

Thirty Years After Graduation, I Spy You in Aisle
    Five / 45

A Brief Natural History of the Girls in the Office / 46

Skinny Dip / 48

Mad / 49

A Brief Natural History of Women

You Come Here Often

And often alone since your best friend joined AA, though she still calls you on the regular to remind you about her sobriety and how grateful she is to wake up in the morning without a SWAT team swarming her brain. She swears you to secrecy, *promise not to tell?,* before she tells you about a woman in her group who, since getting sober, often has sex dreams in Technicolor about a bag boy at Wegmans who's half her age—hell, he's younger than her youngest son—and now the woman can't look the bag boy in the face when he says, *hello, may I be of some assistance,* without thinking of fur handcuffs and the word *throb*, and your best friend tells you again that you can't tell anyone, not a soul, and of course you don't because who would you tell?

You come here often and often you wonder why you do. The bar stinks of smoke and polyester BO from the softball teams that hang out here from April to November; the draft beer is always flat. Also, the television chops characters into legless torsos and topless legs, and unless the Phillies are playing, the television is always tuned to a *Law and Order* episode and there's something about a legless/headless Lennie Briscoe that always undoes you, maybe because Lennie, like your brother, is dead but lives on and on in reruns.

You come here so often that Jeff the Bartender has your beer poured before you sit down, a 20-ounce draft with just enough foam to moustache your upper lip on first swig, enough sparkle to scald your throat. You often think that draft beer is like so many of the men you've known—delicious on first sip, lukewarm-er thereafter, bitter toward the end—and yet you go on ordering drafts hoping that the next one will be different, each sip as delicious as the first one.

You often don't go home because what's home about it anyway—a tiny apartment with a sinkful of dirty dishes, fist of hair clogging the shower's drain, a scraggly orange cat that hangs out on your back stoop, howling his terrible need and hissing when you get too close. Often you find mice guts or a bunny head on the steps, bloody evidence of animal love. Sometimes, but not often, you go home with a guy who smells like your brother did, of warm flannel and corn chips, a guy who has the same nervous curl to his hair. Sometimes you'll smoke a bowl on the roof deck of a rowhouse and stone out on the Philadelphia skyline, on the red PSFS sign burning the night and beyond it the headlights of cars on the bridges stitching states together, on the lightless dark that's the Delaware River. And often, if you're high enough, you'll wonder out loud why it's the Delaware and not the Pennsylvania River or even the New Jersey, and too often the guy will say *Because it's the Delaware, dummy,* instead of tuning into his own high the way your brother would.

Sometimes, but not often, you tell him your brother is dead, that his last words were *Is Sierra Nevada on sale?* Sometimes you wonder how someone can be here one second and gone the next, and often you wish there were reruns.

Always you cry.

A Brief Natural History of How It Is to Be a Girl

We're bleeders or will be. This is what they tell us in a dark room, blinds drawn, rows of desks just so, no bigfoot boys to distract us from the screen. Here is this and this, they tell us: tidy lima bean of uterus, twin snakes of Fallopian tubes into which we'll hatch eggs once a month for forever, such a lovely thing to be a girl, they tell us. Never what we'll need to know, like how not to wear white around that time of the month, how to tie a cardigan to hide where we've leaked, how to plug the leak. How to pray that we'll make it to the bathroom, pray that no one's ripped the Kotex machine off the wall and flung it into one of the stalls for the just-because of it, for the oh-so-damn-good-to-scream-and-throw things days. How it feels to be fizzed-up, a bottle of rage waiting for an occasion to uncork and unload. How our skin will become a radar dish for the hurt of the world, how we'll wish we could unzip ourselves and wear the dull side out. How we're told to hush the *yes* in our girl bodies, so much *yes* in the dark, so much *oh, no*.

A Brief Natural History of Lipstick

We learned to paint our mouths kissable, but were taught not to: by the parish priest, by our mothers, by *Seventeen* magazine. Never on the first date, never more than one boy at a time, never below the neck. We practiced on the mirror and at slumber parties. When boys scratched on the window, we giggled and shivered. Only Lana slipped out, came back smeared and tight-lipped, full-up with stories she wouldn't tell us. At school on Monday, we lipsticked the mirror in the third-floor girl's room: LANA SUCKS. Later we all learned. Later we all did it.

Girl Talk

We're doing shots of Southern Comfort when Sasha finally gets around to telling us about the guy who strolled into the bank that afternoon naked as the day he was born and said *stick 'em up,* like in the movies or something. *Saddest little pistol I ever saw,* Sasha says, and we all laugh and do another shot while she says that the guy—*get this!*—was Jeff Claiborne's brother, Buzzy, who hasn't been right since the accident though we all used to think he was a little odd back in high school for the way he sashayed down the hall hugging everyone he saw, girls and guys. He sang tenor, too, but he broke every school record in the backstroke, there's that, and he was sweet to me and all the other fat girls. After the accident, Buzzy's car was towed to Stevenson's where it sat in the chain-link pen out back, grille twisted into a lopsided smile. For weeks people went down there to gawk and gossip about the front seat slipcovered in blood and the perfect hole in the windshield that Buzzy made when he rocketed onto the pavement. Graduation Day, the principal himself drove over to the Claiborne's to hand Buzzy his diploma, a piece of paper that meant nothing to him, while Mr. and Mrs. Claiborne smiled on. Buzzy spends most days now on the front porch wrapped in a blanket shouting *fuck* and *shit* and *cunt* at the cars that honk by but don't stop, and I've thought about visiting him, even dreamed that he'd come out of his fog and remember me and that time in the men's room of the Burger Chef: the Levi jacket I knelt on and the salty ache of him, how he smelled a little like lavender.

A Brief Natural History of Mothers

We keep the car radio tuned low to the cornball guy in Detroit who plays blue-hair music and tosses silly questions like softballs at people who are supposed to be famous—*What kind of cat would you be if you could be a cat*?—because considering life as a cat is better than thinking about the rotting linoleum in the kitchen and the rosary of ants that live there, about the weight we gained with each of our kids, the pillow of flesh plumping up the wasp waists we had in the wedding photos, the dresses we starved to fit into and how we stood by our soon-to-be husbands bug-eyed and dizzy with hunger and said *I do* to the men we can't bear to think about now, the bars they go to after second shift lets out, the tables of women who smell like whiskey or roses instead of baby pee and furniture spray, and so we crank up the radio and sing along loud though we don't know any of the words.

Reunion

after John Cheever

The last time I saw my mother, she was standing in Penn Station under the arrivals and departures board wearing a wool cardigan buttoned to her throat. It was 5:38 p.m. in late July, 94 degrees outside, but my mother seemed oblivious to both the heat and the mad crash of commuters.

I approached her from the side, the way you would a feral cat. She looked thinner than the last time I'd seen her, the bones in her wrists knobbed under the rolled cuffs. Her face was still unwrinkled. She still wore red lipstick.

"Hello," I said.

She turned her head slowly and studied me for a few seconds before she smiled. "Oh," she said. "Hannah." Her voice was breathier than I remembered, vowels drawn out. She didn't sound surprised to see me.

She gestured at the list of destinations. "Tell me, please: what is a *Metuchen*?"

This was a game we used to play on her okay days. We'd pick an obscure word from that morning's newspaper and spend the dinner hour making up a definition. Whoever came up with the cleverest was the winner, though there never was a real prize.

"What are you doing here?" I asked.

She smiled. Her front right tooth was chipped. It made her look younger.

"A metal vessel for preparing goulash," she said. "Your turn."

The flip board whirred and clicked. My train was announced. The line grew wider and longer, aimed itself at the dark opening that led to the track. If I wanted a seat, I needed to get in line now. Say goodbye. Ask her to write down a phone number, maybe, or an address.

"A percussion instrument," I said. "A cross between a snare drum and tympani."

"Excellent!" she said. She sounded so delighted that I found myself saying *sure, yeah* when she asked me if I had time for a cup of coffee.

*

We ordered at a counter. I offered to pay and she didn't say no. We sat in a booth near the back. The curved seats were made out of something hard and orange. It was a dismal place, humid with a mustard yellow light.

My mother took the cover off her coffee sniffed it. "Burned," she said. She shook a sugar pack into her cup. She did that four more times before giving her coffee a stir. Only then did she take a sip. "Not bad."

I once dated this guy who did the exact same thing. Whenever he finished a piece of pie, he all but licked the plate clean. On our first date, he told me he was in recovery. We'd been fixed up by a mutual friend who knew we both loved books. We had fun for a while, then he called to tell me he couldn't see me anymore. *Too dangerous*, he said. When I asked him to explain, he hung up on me.

My mother nodded to the music threading through the speakers. I sipped my coffee. It was bitter and weak.

"I love this song," she said. "Don't you love this song?"

"I don't know this song," I said.

"Sure, you do!" she said, filling in on the chorus with her alto harmony. She could still sing. In spite of everything, she still had that voice.

I picked up her stir stick and fiddled with it. "How have you been?"

"Oh," she said, "here and there."

She heard me say *how*. I know she did.

"That's good," I said. "So what brings you here?"

"This and that," she said. She leaned in close and whispered, "Don't look now, but that man at the cash register? He's not wearing any underwear."

It was the kind of thing she noticed, the odd detail that would often prove to be telling about that person or thing. *He has shifty hands*, is what she said about an old boyfriend. *In and out of his pockets, always moving.*

I didn't look.

"A man," she said. "But it's not what you think! It's business. He owns a supper club, and I sang for him. You know, an . . . "

She paused.

"Audition?" I said.

"Yes. An audition," she said. "Exactly. See here." She shoved a crumpled business card across the table: *The Two-Fifty-Two Saloon*, it said. Then again, she could have picked up this card anywhere, from the ground or a trashcan where someone had tossed it.

It wouldn't be the first time she'd imagined something. "Are you sure, Mother?" I meant it gently, but it came out all wrong and she heard it.

"*Sure?*" she said. "What do you mean, *sure?*"

The man two tables over looked up from his coffee. I could ask her to tell me about the audition and she would. She would tell me about the spotlight, the out-of-tune piano, the man who looked bored until she started to sing. How her hands shook no matter how many times she'd done this. She'd tell me all this as though it had happened, make me believe in the thing as much as she did.

Another fairy tale, full of unhappily-ever-afters.

I crumpled up my napkin and stuffed it into my half-empty coffee cup. "I have a train to catch," I said. That much was real. She walked with me as far as the departures and arrival board and told me she would say goodbye here. She said she liked to picture the trains

coming and going, the people on them. I imagined she saw herself on each of them, constructing a life for herself complete with props and a better daughter.
"I'll send you tickets when I open," she said. "Good seats, up front, okay?"

Sure, I said.

Before I went down the stairs, I turned to look at her staring up at the flip board, and that was the last time I saw my mother.

Oh, the Water

You're across the bar jingling quarters in your cupped palm, blue-faced from the light of the jukebox, looking for songs that aren't there when a woman wearing a purple tutu on her head says she'll read my palm for a shot and a beer.

Songs you sang to the baby while you rocked around the living room in the evening. Twilight Dance Party, you called it, even in the summer when the sun was still high.

Water hands, says Tutu Lady. *Long palms and fingers, see that? Soft to the touch.* Damp, too, though it's chilly in here, sealed away from the sun's punishment. We're somewhere in Arizona, one hundred ten today, enough to dizzy-up the blood.

*

In the desert, water is a mirage. You drive and drive toward a lake that evaporates.

But water is water, real or imagined, and hot is hot, dry or not.

*

Start me up, Mick sings. *Never stop*. A song you'd never sing to a baby.

*

Tutu Lady says I'm lucky, my lifeline's strong and long the way her mother's was. Cancer ate her up from the inside out, but okay, her mother was ninety and tired, ready to move onto the next thing.

*

On the road, the only rules are no rules: No four-lane highways, no fast food joints, no campgrounds with RV hookups and game rooms. What we save on lodging and showers, we blow on drinks in shitty bars, the shittier the better. Windows curtained in dusty neon, a couple of smokers huddled around the front door, names with a certain seediness: Joe's Down Low, Frank's Dive, Thelma's Cellar. When people ask where we're headed, we say Nowhere.

Sounds like you're running from something, said the man at the bar in New Mexico. *Not to.*

*

There's a mark on my heart line, a little red square below the finger where I used to wear my wedding ring before I lost it swimming laps. I lied and said it was stolen, promised I'd fill out the insurance forms.

I never did. I swam more laps. Oh, the water.

*

We used to wait until 5 o'clock, but lately we're barely past lunch when we start to drink. In the car, our silences are full of sharp things we aim at the raw spots. Booze is balm for the scraped parts.

Something happened, says Tutu Lady tracing the square with her fingernail. *Something hurts.*

*

Who's a good boy, you used to say. Like he was a pet, the same silly voice you used for the cat. *Me*! he'd squeal. *Who's a burrito*? you'd say, try to wrap him in a towel to rub him dry. But he'd run around wet, slippery as a bar of soap and just as hard to grab, daring you to chase him. The fun you had while I was stuck scrubbing out the tub, swabbing the floor where the water had puddled.

The one time I didn't.

*

At some point, you'll slide your last quarter in the jukebox and come back to me. We'll drink each other close, kiss or hold hands, remember what it was like to like each other before we forget again.

The Thing With Feathers

Dear red-headed lady:
Thank you for not asking why I was crying.

Dear red-headed lady outside the bar:
If I told you I never cried, I'd be lying. Something I'm trying to grow out of.

Dear red-headed lady who offered to share your umbrella when it started to rain:
Sometimes I cry on Monday when the six of us and Karen sit in a Sunday school room in the basement of a church smelling of furniture polish and urine. We sit in a circle and drink bitter coffee, tell stories that scald the tongue.

We do this every Monday before the old, bad habits we may have skidded toward during the weekend can take hold.

Dear red-headed lady whose hair smelled of smoke and roses:
Eunice my bus driver blames her husband's cancer on the cigars he smoked during Thursday night poker games with the guys from the line at Kodak. The Lord is your shepherd, I tell her. The walls at group are full up with him, stick figures watching over glued-on blobs of cotton that I believe to be sheep. The Lord is my shepherd, block letters in orange crayon. His wayward flock.

Dear red-headed umbrella lady who gave me a cigarette and a pack of matches when your lighter wouldn't light:
I didn't cry this morning, but Denise did when Karen made us share what we're thankful for. *I'm alive*, Denise said, and started to cry. Denise, who used to make a living with her fists. You can see it in the way she sits, like she's waiting for the bell to signal the next round. How she glares at the floor like it's going to rise up and slap her upside the head.

Denise, who never cries.

When the circle got around to me, I said I'm glad I don't have cancer, and someone—I think it was Susan—said *amen*.

Dear lady of the cigarette smoke, umbrella of roses:
There are days I wish I had cancer, too, something fatal and final so I could give myself up to the leaving instead of what Karen calls the business of living.

I'm bankrupt. I'm alive.

Dear lady who I hope doesn't have the cancer you get from red hair dye:
My name is Ada, and I'm an alcoholic.

Dear kind lady, dear you whose name I wish I knew:
Why didn't I go with you, step under the spokes of your umbrella and walk the block or so to the bus stop?

Next Monday, I'll tell the group that I did. Karen says we live in the almost but if we can stay on the side of the street where the sun shines, we'll be okay.

I'll say *almost* and they'll clap for me. I will say I almost walked past you instead of into the bar.

Dear lady who looks like she might be a Patti or a Sandi:

She was wearing pajamas printed all over in calico cats wearing fuzzy pink slippers. There were white lights threaded through the trees outside of the bar where I parked. She was sleeping in her booster seat, but I said to wait here, honey, mommy will be right back, the way I always did. One or two was all, enough to quench my thirst.

Dear Patti or Sandi:

What I am is a liar. I will tell you that I had two drinks when I had five. I will say they were weak drinks when they were double shots. I will sit in that circle on Monday and tell the story about how I dream that I'm riding a bus with my daughter. Karen will say that to dream her alive again is a good thing, a hopeful thing. Hope is the thing with feathers, she likes to say. Hope should perch in our soul and sing to us.

A Brief Natural History of Our Fathers

Our fathers rise at 5 and whistle out the door carrying thermoses of black coffee and lunches our mothers have packed for them—bags of corn chips that fat up the blood and sandwiches made of meat and cheese. Our mothers tuck notes into the wrap of waxed paper promising what they'll do to our fathers later in the dark.

*

Weekends, our fathers box-step us around the living room or somersault us from their shoulders into the deep end of a swimming pool. Sometimes our fathers will lock themselves away and listen to Tiger games on the radio or slide under cars until they're called to wash up for dinner.

*

Our fathers are *men*. What our mothers say when we ask why our fathers never cook or change diapers. *Restless men*, they say. Later they'll say it with rolled eyes, but only in the evening after a couple of highballs have unlatched their tongues. *Men*, they will say. Our only inheritance.

*

On summer nights our fathers gather with other fathers in back yards to drink and bitch about the asshole foreman, the infernal factory clatter. Enough beer and they brag about the muscle cars they're building, the flex and thrum of their big engines.

*

Some of our fathers die drunk in head-ons or face down on the factory floor, their rotted hearts knotted as pine trees. Some of our fathers carry their coffins and try not to cry.

*

Our fathers circle the padlocked gate of the Ford plant carrying signs they shake at the scabs who have stolen their jobs. Our fathers walk in snow and rain, raise clenched fists at the cars that honk past them. They stay out late drinking beer, roll home long after we're in bed.

*

Our fathers are shut down, laid off. They drink beer from cans that they crush in their hands and leave on the coffee table for us to clean up. They watch game shows and talk shows where movie stars share photos of the dogs they buy through the mail and fly first class from Tokyo. Our mothers tiptoe around our fathers, steer clear of their simmer and filth. They whisper over the slosh of the dishwasher about how hard it is for a man not to work.

*

After the Ford plant closes, our fathers go back to school at night. Shaved raw and choked by neckties, they stare down the glare of computer screens. Other fathers disappear into the dark bars downtown, lit by the flicker of TV screens and the thunder of fights. Sometimes the door will open and burp out the smell of beer and sweat and bullshit.

*

We grow up, go away, marry men who are not our fathers, men with soft hands and clean fingernails. Men who read stories to their daughters about cloth rabbits and moons and spiders that die alone.

*

Out fathers get old and then older. Soon enough they're headlights on a wall, there and gone. Shadows, then ghosts.

That Girl

we used to laugh at, that girl who walked the hallways head-down, cold-shouldered by lockers, who blistered her fingers twisting Kleenex into flowers for homecoming floats the cool girls would ride on

yeah, that girl

was nobody we knew until she went missing and then we remembered how in first grade she peed a puddle that spread and smelled of cheese and fish and scattered the class until the janitor showed up with a broom and a pail of red dust, remembered the Show and Tell in fifth grade when she shared the broken glass she'd found on the street and swore it was amber, remembered how some guys at our high school spray-painted her name across the stadium bleachers where they used to screw her and how they laughed at her afterward

god, that girl

will be winched-up blue and broken from a lake, will live on forever as a yearbook picture on a TV screen, dust of blush, lipstick pinking her mouth, nobody we remember

that girl was nobody

we knew.

A Brief Natural History of The Other Woman

I'm playing Goldilocks to your Papa Bear when the boats rev up again. Four days they've been searching, the divers and the hooks that bring up nothing. Four nights I've been sleeping in your bed listening in while you call Mama Bear to check up on Baby: *Out of town, business again.* Afterward, you're still and opaque as the lake, a sad landscape I ache to row, imagine how each pull of the oars would leave a wake of holes but we're running low on Cointreau. Remember how I used to dip my fingers in tequila and let you suck them, swallow me up to the second knuckle? I was lemon, I was salt. Now we sip from polite glasses and watch while the winch groans up a tangle of seaweed and feet, face blue as a bruise, and though we know the dead can't resurrect no matter how many stones you roll back, no matter how lusty the hallelujahs, we bow our heads. Only the lake will repair itself, seal over what's been disturbed.

A Brief Natural History of Babies, Because

We had them because the rubber broke while hot and heavy in the backseat of the drive-in, because ginger-ale was an old wives' tale. Because there was no morning-after pill, not yet, no abortion that wasn't back-alley Detroit or two weeks in Sweden. We had them because we were nice girls who refused to tuck rubbers in the coin purse of our billfolds, because we were okay with the whispers—in the aisles of the A&P or later at graduation when we crossed the stage with a belly out to here—because we were mostly okay with all of it until the afternoon of the baby shower when we passed joints and a warm bottle of André and cried a little about all the life we'd never get to live because, face it, we were girls who had to have them.

In Real Life

Both she and Janie sign contracts, but Janie chickens out at the last minute, claiming summer school and a boyfriend, so in the end, she takes the bus up there alone, her stuff spread across two seats. Her mother is full of stories about girls alone on buses, the trouble they get into with men who get funny with them and get off at the next stop, how real life is exactly like those confession magazines she used to read, where the men get to be light and fast as jackrabbits and the women trudge and stumble.

The place is nothing much, nothing like the pictures the recruiter had shared of boats in blue water, white-coated waiters delivering trays of drinks to women in bikinis stretched out on chaise lounges next to a swimming pool. The pool in real life is hardly bigger than a bathtub with water the color of a bruise. But Syl, the girl she rooms with, says give it a few weeks, it'll pep up, and in the meantime, try to enjoy it.

The third night, Syl loans her some hussy shoes and gets her all gussied up in a top down to there, a skirt up to here. And no lipstick, but heavy on the eyeliner. Syl says women who wear eyeliner mean business. They drive to a dump of a bar on a road crowded by fir trees where the bartender doesn't card her and pours double drinks for single shot money. After two drinks, a fog sets in. The jukebox plays the same songs that spun her through senior year; a cue stick scatters balls like molecules. H_2O is water, but CO is poison, something she remembers from chemistry class. It seemed important at the time to understand the difference between what could kill her and what would save her.

After lunch shift the next day, she buys a postcard of the long-dead bear whose spirit still haunts the place, something she'll laugh at until her comb mysteriously disappears from the dresser where she left it. In two weeks, she'll be able to balance a tray of martinis on her fingertips, deliver each drink without spilling. In three weeks, she'll sleep with a bartender who promises to pull out in time and doesn't.

Having a ball, she writes. *Wish you were here.*

All We Wanted

It was Juanita's job to check each plate for a single strand of hair or, god forbid, a dead fly before we stacked them three deep on trays and carried them on our shoulders up a steep flight of stairs. Once she dropped a cigarette ash on a slab of prime rib and swiped it with a towel until you couldn't tell what was meat and not. Had we done that, she would have given us what-for, made us stay late to scrub down the inside of the walk-in cooler. Which was fine with us. We'd sneak a six-pack in there and a bottle of vodka that we'd pass back and forth. We'd help ourselves to handfuls of fresh shrimp from a plastic can and call it dinner. We'd leave that cooler gleaming, leave it drunk, stopping long enough to shuck our shoes before heading out to dance. Eight hours on our feet and all we wanted was to dance.

Your Life as a Bottle

Closing time, you hang out with the dishwashers who keep a bottle tucked behind the toilet tank in the employee's restroom, something rotgut and lowdown that tastes of Lysol and piss. A shot or two does the trick, makes it so you don't hate the cute girls with good teeth and cleavage delivering last-call martinis to rich guys while you're stuck in the kitchen refilling condiments. You're superstitious enough to pinch salt over your shoulder whenever you spill it, fool enough to whisper a wish. You marry your ketchups in a little ceremony—*Who takes this woman*—though it's less a commitment and more like pickup sex, random bottles tipped together lip to lip, each bleeding quick and urgent into the other while their caps stew clean in scalding water. Later you'll head to a bar where you'll drink yourself pretty under the black light of the dance floor. Later you'll find somebody to tip yourself into, an anybody who will empty you out and leave you clean.

A Brief Natural History of the Automobile

Your father insists that you pray daily to Henry Ford, the patron saint of Michigan who puts steak on the table and keeps sneakers on your feet, but you're not willing to die for him. It's all because of Henry Ford and his automobiles that the Cubans are pointing their missiles at Detroit *right now*, according to your geography teacher. The Cubans will aim their bombs *right here,* she says, jabbing at the wall map of Michigan, its vulnerable thumb. They'll shoot them at the Ambassador Bridge and Tiger Stadium and at the beating steel heart of the River Rouge Ford plant and blast it all into a pile of dust.

You decide you don't want to die without doing it, though you're not clear on what *it* is. You suspect it has something to do with boys and what Donald Spatts does to you in the AV room. Donald Spatts has palms like swamps and too much spit in his mouth, but you let him press you up against the shelves of filmstrips and slide his tongue between your teeth. Afterward he cracks his knuckles and says, boy, what he'd like to do to those Commies.

Years from now, Donald Spatts will die in Vietnam, in a village that's not on any map. His twelfth-grade face will smile out forever from the trophy case in the high school lobby.

You are riding on top of a snow-white 1967 Impala convertible, waving to the nearly empty street as if twisting a light bulb. Your driver, a guy from the dealership, has patent leather hair and sneers when you decline his offer of a cigarette. You suspect he would rather be driving Delores Hiser ("Best Body"), who thinks a bachelor's degree is something a college awards to unmarried men, or Betsy Gilchrist ("Most Fun on a Date"). Your driver is not impressed that you were voted "Most Likely to Succeed." This is apparent from the way he brakes too suddenly and corners too fast, forcing you to plant the tips of your imitation satin slippers into the crevice of the seat so you don't roll over like the Titanic while you wave and smile.

You do it for the first time in the backseat of your '70 Mustang, a graduation present from your father. You're nineteen, it's time. You do it with a French-Canadian hockey player who likes to caress your chrome bumpers with hands the size of shovels. You like how his hands spread you across the buttery leather of the backseat. Except for *puck* and *hello*, he speaks no English, which is fine. You like to drive in silence.

You fall for a man who names his cars after Greek gods and croons Sinatra tunes while he paste-waxes their bodies. Like you, he loves driving anywhere and nowhere. You study maps at gas stations on backroads while he shows off his '66 GTO to the mechanics who migrate like Crusaders to the car. While they worship at the altar of the engine, you follow blue highways with your forefinger, tracing the route you'll never take to Mexico.

Your husband whistles as he folds you into his Corvette and tells you to hold on for the ride of your life. At the hospital, you're wheeled into a dark room, away from your husband, your unindicted co-conspirator.

Headlights are shined into your eyes; a semi rolls over your stomach. While you push out a human, your husband hands out cigars and swaps car stories with two other men in the waiting room.

You're no longer a sports car but a utility vehicle whose body is chipped and dinged. You have gray roots and frown lines and ten pounds that won't go away. Your best friend is your hairstylist who calls you *honey* and *girlfriend* and has sworn a blood oath to tell you whenever you have chin hair.

Your daughter endures you. She slumps in the passenger seat, refusing to speak. The pediatrician tells you not to worry, it's a phase she'll grow out of. She'd rather drive with her father who lets her steer and never says no.

Your husband no longer goes to the barber, but he meets weekly with his stylist, a woman who shellacs his hair into an aerodynamic fin that hides his bald spot. Your husband stands in the mirror, studying his stomach. He begins to wear cologne. You begin to snoop. You find a copy of *The Kama Sutra for Dummies* in his briefcase, "from your little Mercedes with *beaucoup* love."

You understand completely. Your husband has always wanted a Mercedes, now he's found himself a good used one.

Your car dies on a dark night, on a road with no cell service, so you must walk. Your shoes pinch and your right ankle cracks, but the air is sweet with hickory smoke and roses. Maybe you'll invest in some comfortable shoes and an iPod, teach yourself French in fifteen easy lessons. Maybe you'll walk across France. Maybe you'll learn to say *non*.

Maybe, maybe, maybe you sing as you walk. Not away anymore, but toward something you sense is there.

Henry Ford est mort. Vive Henry Ford

Saginaw

That summer I hung out with the lifers, girls who'd mastered the four-plate carry and the stink eye for guys with fast hands. We drank beer at a dive bar between shifts, played darts or pool until dinner. I punched in and folded napkins into swans and sharks and sailor hats. The cook called me a fat cunt, and no one said *please* or *thank you*. I served and smiled. I was a fish under ice, swimming toward a light. So many slow mornings. So much traffic behind me and in front of me, the stoplight always stuck on red.

Other Tongues

I decided to learn French so I could finally talk about my brother. I wanted his death to feel distant, more like a movie I could turn off when it got too sad. And for months I'd been too sad and in the most ridiculous places—the vegetable aisle of the grocery store, say, where I'd be feeling up avocados, pressing their little green buttons to test for ripeness, and I'd get so choked up I thought I'd suffocate. The therapist I was seeing said the grief I'd stuffed down probably wanted out, and I immediately thought of the horror movie my brother and I had watched a long time ago, about some amphibious pet that had been flushed down a city toilet and was only now crawling up out of the sewer, monstrous and nuclear and ready to wreak revenge.

The French class was cheap and close by. Once a week I'd show up at the elementary school a couple blocks from me with my notebook and the "textbook" I'd been given, stapled sheets that smelled of ink and booze and cigarettes because the teacher liked to duck out for a smoke whenever we broke into conversational groups. He was actually French-Canadian, but he'd lived in Paris for several years where he worked as a copyeditor for *les journals* and had subsequently been fired when the French, like everyone else, started reading *les journals* on line for free. I liked that he called it what it was—a firing—unlike here in the U.S. where they try to clean everything up to make it sound not as horrible as it is. *Downsizing. Rightsizing. Passed away*, instead of dead, like the person has slipped into another dimension to live for a while.

41

The classroom was full of little desks we stuffed ourselves into and copied what our teacher, Monsieur Bernard, wrote on the blackboard. He had funny handwriting, s's looked like f's so that "sister" was *foeur* and *suis* was *fuis*. Also, he liked to draw little stick figures to illustrate what he was talking about whenever we looked puzzled: *le chien et le chat*, though *le chat* was twice as big as *le chien* and had *les dents de lion*, like the dingy orange stray that yowled around my back door and bit me whenever I was slow to feed him. He'd shown up months ago, right after my brother was killed, so I let him stick around. Once he snarfed all the food in the dish and strutted over and peed on my leg. Whenever I tried to pet him, he bucked and hissed. I understood that. I'd felt the same way at my brother's funeral whenever someone tried to hug me and tell me things like *God's will* or *this, too, will pass*.

By the sixth week, we were down to a handful of people, the way it always is with classes. People show up shiny and enthusiastic with brand new notebooks, each blank page a new beginning that lasts until the pages are dirtied by crossouts and then it's all about failure again, everything you tried to do and couldn't. I kept showing up because French shoved the monster out of my head for the ninety minutes I was there, like having new, quiet tenants living above me instead of crappy frat boys.

On this night, there were only three of us: Marie, a woman with blue hair who muttered to herself, and Bob the accountant who had been rechristened Ro-BEAR during the first class. We waited fifteen minutes and still no Monsieur Bernard. The Spanish class next door was shouting replies to the questions I couldn't hear—TACOS! QUESADILLAS!—and I was suddenly hungry though I'd eaten a pack of salted peanuts right before I came.

After fifteen minutes, Marie left so it was only Robert and me. He clicked his ballpoint pen and I studied the turkeys the kids had made by tracing their hands and coloring in the finger/feathers. There were a lot of rainbow flags or red, white and blue turkeys. The ones my brother and I had made were tame by comparison, brown and grey and dull as a November sky, and yet my mother had taped them to the refrigerator where they stayed for decades. After the funeral, I tried to unpeel my brother's turkey from the refrigerator, but the paper crumbled and tore.

The Spanish class was on ENCHILADAS! when a woman came in, Annie, she said she was, the administrator for adult education. She was red-eyed like she'd been crying or was tired. She said Monsieur Bernard was unable to meet with us tonight or ever again, for that matter, and she would process whatever refund was owed us and mail a check ASAP.

For weeks, I googled his name and found nothing about him, so I've begun making up stories to tell the orange cat who stops by for breakfast now: A Russian spy, a deadbeat dad, and the latest tale, a murder. The cat loves this one, I can tell. I'm teaching myself the French words for *gun* and *six-pack of beer*, for *holdup* and *convenience store* and *senseless*, but brother, there are no words for the monster that lives on inside me.

A Brief Natural History of *Law and Order*

Tuesday, you're the girl who was raped and stabbed and stuffed into trash bags within eyeshot of two executive high rises on the Upper West Side. The trash bags will lead Briscoe and Green to a suspect, a parks employee whose own mom used to lock him in a closet so she could party in peace

Wednesday, you're the girl on a slab in the morgue, your body dusted in white light. On a break, the suspect brings you a cup of coffee dark as the dirt they'll bury you in. He talks to the scars that hair-and-makeup carved on the curve of your tits. You vow again to study ventriloquism so your tits can talk back.

Thursday, you're the long-gone twin of the dead girl. You wear a pilled cardigan raveling at the elbows and a dark wig that sweats your head, a guilty itch. You swear on a bible to tell the truth, that your sister was a crackhead who blew men in bathrooms for spare change. You sob on the stand, an Emmy worthy performance. The director yells cut and asks for a little less hysteria, please.

Friday, Saturday and Sunday: You sleep in late.

Monday, you're found guilty of killing your twin who was really the good sister.

Tuesday, you're eating lunch in the park when a man in a green uniform hoists two trash bags and tosses them into a dumpster. He wipes his hands and walks toward you, smiling.

Thirty Years After Graduation, I Spy You in Aisle Five

I'd have bet prison, fifteen to life for offing your ex while he slept next to the younger blonde who stole your crown. Or maybe the roller derby, skating endless, sweaty circles alongside women nicknamed Glory Hole and Cuntalingus, girls who'd sharpened their elbows on high school scorn. Or most likely an OD, a quick funeral with a closed casket smothered in flowers smelling of pee and furniture polish, a service where the clueless pastor lists *prudence* as one of your stellar qualities. But here you are alive in Aisle Five shushing a pale something whose fat legs are threaded into a grocery cart full up with jars of baby food the color of what we used to puke up at parties so we could drink more. I should thank you for explaining blow job to me, for slipping me that baggie full of pills that hotted up my heart until I burned a furnace of calories and finally got skinny. Instead we talk about Lucy, Sherry, Pam: *Cancer, a stroke, a jealous lover.* Once I dreamed they were waving from a boat pulling away from the shore. I don't know where I thought you were. Driving, I suppose.

A Brief Natural History of the Girls in the Office

Early on, the engagements and weddings and after that, the babies and the christenings and first communions. Each time we passed a white envelope from desk to desk, whatever we could spare, a buck or two, five if it was payday and we were feeling flush. Sometimes there was cake, and we'd flip a coin for the corner piece with the heap of sugared roses that went down sweetly with just the right ache.

Later on, potluck lunches together in the breakroom where we learned to like Inez's potato salad with its pucker of onion, Melinda's tuna noodle casserole crusted with Saltines, the shortbread cookies Judy made from a recipe that was willed to her by her Scots grandmother. Sometimes, and only on Fridays, we sneaked in a bottle of something bubbly to sweeten our iced tea on last break, warm us up for the weekend ahead.

Soon enough, the sorrow. The kids moved out and never called. Parents died and husbands left us for women with clear skin and stomachs unpouched by babies. Cancer helped itself to breasts and ovaries, chemo took what was left of the feeling in fingers and toes, took the hair we'd spent our lives fussing with. We passed the envelope again, this time for flowers, and said what the hell. The few of us who were left started bowling together on Wednesdays, pretending the pins we scattered were second wives or the exes who were late again with the support. We pooled coins from our purses and split pitchers of beer afterward, something cheap and yeasty to wash down the baskets of stale potato chips we dipped into ketchup or drowned in malt vinegar. We clicked our plastic cups together before the first sip, saying *one more week*.

Sometimes we closed down the bar and lingered in the parking lot, watched bugs swarm and bump up against the blue lights. Sometimes we went out for breakfast and cried into our over-easies, hold-the-toast. Sometimes we wondered who would pass the envelope for us.

Skinny Dip

We do it on nights when the stars hang low and heavy, ripe fruit in a black bowl of sky, nights when we're so stoned we make bets about when the stars will fall on us. We're always stoned, so what? The guy from Detroit is always the first to take off his pants, the last to jump in. *Snakes,* he says. Or eels. He swims head-out like a dog, coughs water, a pot smoker's wet hack. Years from now the cops will find him in a car trunk, shot once through the head, the pound of cocaine he was carrying long gone. For years I'll mouth-to-mouth him back to life, I'll dream him awake. He floats face up forever in a stew of stars, a body at rest patiently waiting.

Mad

Kat goes missing again, but not really. She's where she usually is—passed out, pants on backward, in the Wawa parking lot. Because this is her third or fourth offense, the dean of students summons her parents who drive eight hours through a freak April snowstorm. This is how much they love her, this is how much they want her to get well. *You kids*, her mother used to say, whenever one of them did something that baffled her. But there is no more *you kids,* no Kit or Kitten or Katie, only the Katherine in several official-looking documents the dean shares with her parents: *Academic probation, mandatory counseling.* Her parents bookend her, nodding agreement. The dean of students looks smug and shiny as an eggplant.

The therapist she's sentenced to is bearded, upholstered in wool and corduroy. His office is windowless and dark with two armchairs that itch. He tells her to call him Joe, but she doesn't feel like talking, so they read instead: psychology magazines with covers that shout about big emotions and the power of boundaries, or old issues of *Mad* that bring back her brother, how he'd named the family canary Alfred E. Neuman and tried to teach it to belch harmony to "It's a Gas." She wanted to play the record at his funeral, but her mother said absolutely not and had gone with hymns instead, full of God and mighty fortresses that Kat pretended to sing along with.

Her heart is a stone. When she walks across campus, she feels neon-lit: The Sister of the Guy Who Was Murdered at the Wawa. She is thirsty all the time.

On their fourth Friday, Joe hands her a box of crayons and some paper and asks her to draw a happy place, her idea of a heaven. She pauses for a second then sketches in tables, hanging plants, a birdcage in the window. A row of stools, three tiers of liquor bottles rising like a choir. Joe says, *Birds? In a bar?* "Wild canaries," she says. Birds that sing sweetly, the way her brother sang in the shower or when he harmonized on Happy Birthday. She hopes his soul flew up out of him when he was shot

Maybe open up the cage? Joe says, so she does. And, oh, what a wild bird can do when set loose indoors. Such madness. Such damage.

Acknowledgments

Grateful acknowledgment is made to the editors of the following journals who published these stories, or earlier versions of them:

100-Word Story: "A Brief Natural History of Lipstick" as "Lipstick"

Cleaver: "A Brief Natural History of Our Fathers"

Emerge Literary Journal: "Saginaw"

Empty House Press: "Oh, the Water"

Five South: "A Brief Natural History of How It Is to Be a Girl" as "To Be a Girl"

Fictive Dream: "Girl Talk"

Fractured Lit: "Mad" and "Thirty Years After Graduation, I Spy You in Aisle Five"

Milk Candy Review: "All We Wanted" and "A Brief Natural History of the Girls in the Office"

New World Writing: "A Brief Natural History of *Law and Order*" and "Skinny Dip"

Pithead Chapel and *Best Microfiction 2022:* "My Life as a Bottle" and "Reunion"

Smokelong Quarterly: "A Brief Natural History of the Automobile" and "The Thing With Feathers"

South Florida Poetry Journal: "You Come Here Often"

The Journal: "Other Tongues"

Trampset: "In Real Life"

X-Ray Lit: "That Girl"

So much gratitude to all the teachers whose prompts and encouragement led to so many of these stories: Sara Lippmann, Meg Pokrass, Nancy Stohlman, Tommy Dean, and Kathy Fish.

Thanks to friends for always being there: Sarah Cedeno, Jennifer Litt, Anne Panning and Darby Knox.

For Allison Blevins and the team at Harbor Editions, thanks for everything.

Sarah Freligh is the author of five books, including *Sad Math*, winner of the 2014 Moon City Press Poetry Prize and the 2015 Whirling Prize from the University of Indianapolis, and *We*, published by Harbor Editions in 2021. Recent work has appeared in the *Wigleaf 50*, *New Micro: Exceptionally Short Fiction* (Norton 2018), *Best Microfiction* (2019-22), and *Best Small Fiction* 2022. Among her awards are poetry fellowships from the National Endowment for the Arts and the Saltonstall Foundation.

Milton Keynes UK
Ingram Content Group UK Ltd.
UKHW011957040923
428043UK00005B/527